The Creepside

By
David Owens JR

These stories were written and performed by myself and is an extension of myself as an artist. These stories can be heard through spotify and thus why there are such different writing styles. It's meant to be read out loud by a campfire or to your children as a bedtime story!

(please don't do that)

Index

Mortality
the quality or state of being mortal

Humans are weird. I am told that I am human although I do not feel like one. I mean I breathe, I eat and I feel pain and stuff but I do not feel human. I can't feel emotions but I can fake them very well. I can smile at babies and puppies but normally that follows with the drowning thoughts of stomping them under the heel of my boot. The crunch of their skulls and the squish of the visceral is just so satisfying. Seriously. Try it..

Not all of us are as blessed as I am. For you see I am immortal. I've been shot, stabbed, poisoned, had cancer, ect,ect. I simply just can't die. As long as i can remember i've been bored with the living population. If you can tell by the above paragraph I am a bit of a psychopath. I became one in my late 20's. Shortly after the passing of my dear elizabeth.
Elizabeth was my pet lobster. One day she is in her tank enjoying her slice of cod and the next day she is bright red and

smothered in garlic butter. Oh how life just throws you these curveballs.

It all started with my wife. Yes, somebody loved me enough to marry me but this story isn't about her mistakes it's about my achievements. She was sleeping in bed. A king size we got for a good price at the local discount store. There she was. Still sleeping. Chest gently going up and down to the rhythm pattern of her damn snoring that has kept me up for many a night. Shellfish and garlic butter still stained my tongue and I was breathing heavily. The veins in my neck swole. I could hear my heart in my ears. I couldn't stop it. I didn't want to stop it.

I jumped on top of her pinning my wife to our bed. I grabbed a pillow to muffle her screams of terror. As I raised the lobster claw high above my head I couldn't help but to think. I wonder how hard I have to stab to get this through her skull. Not completely confident in the structural integrity of a cooked lobster claw, I removed the pillow. As she tries to let out a scream I shove the claw in her mouth. I pushed it as hard as I could and I could feel her jaw break under the immense pressure. Then it couldn't go any further. Still alive I panicked and punched the claw as hard as I could. The gut wrenching sound of her bone and flesh squelched and echoed through my ears. Then silence. I rolled off of her and layed next to her body until I heard it. "Daddy?"

Fuck. caroline. My daughter. I look across the room to see her in her soft fuzzy pink pajamas standing in the open doorway. "Is mommy ok?" she said with a tired concern in her voice. "Come on my darling time to go to bed". I take her by her hand and walk her to her room. She takes two steps in front of me then it happens. I pick her up to screams and squeals. I shush her as I wrap my arm around her neck and pulled. The snap indicates that she will tell nobody of what has happened here tonight.

Was I angry when I killed my family? No. I was bored. Bored of going to those horrible plays and piano recitals. Bored of dinner parties with the neighbors and their boring stories of their trip to flagstaff. There is nothing fun about flagstaff karen. Most of all I was bored of holding back. Since I let loose life has been a gas. I do what I want when I want.

Now i dont do anything tasteless like rape or pedophilia. Oh no no no my poison is feeling the last beat of the heart in whatever victim I choose. Which brings me to my next adventure.
My third kill. And to this date it was my most dangerous and satisfying kill. Detective french. Oh how I miss the hunt between us. As you can imagine this was not easy as I had to set my old life on fire to not raise suspicion. Some burns here and a bruise there with a side of hysterical crying got me scott free with any authority figure. That is except for detective french. He was one of those big city detectives in a small town, pains in my asses. He thought he was soooo smart.

Even going as far as to follow me to my physical therapy appointments and to the grocery store. Money was his theory. If he would have done his research he would have known that I was comfortable and had no debt. I didn't need money. I needed satisfaction and now like with most drugs I crave more.

It was around this time I was diagnosed with stage 4 lung cancer. All this did was push the need to kill to new levels. So I began to stalk. It wasn't hard to do. He drove a mid 2000"s crown vic. Like the fucking cop he was. I learned after he is done for the day he goes straight to a local watering hole to drown his sorrows in a tall glass of regret of not being able to catch me. Afterwards he drives home to a modest cottage and a busy residential street. The house is dark until he gets home. He then sits in front of the idiot tube until he eventually goes upstairs and god knows i do not what to think he does up there.i deduced that he lived alone. Probably divorced. Then it happened one night during my stake out. A woman shows up. Blonde hair. Skinny. Leopard print mini skirt. Tacky red tube top. The only problem is she never left. I know, I was there all night. The next day despite no sleep I decided to step inside of his house after he left for work bright and early. Figured i could send him a message with his little lady friend but oh no. how wrong I was. The house was empty. Aside from needing an interior designer it was normal. I ventured upstairs and was pleasantly surprised. There she was. Tied upside down with a tub under her. Bleeding her dry. As one sick fuck to another. This was art.

Now I have him. I had to do some prep work. While in the house I took pictures of the entire house and every room. Including his bloody girlfriend. Then I went home only to be interrupted at my apartment door by none other than detective french himself. "So where have you been all night?" he says with a stern attitude. "My dear man, I was at the gravesite of my beloved, then I went to kimo. Would you please leave me alone? ``I said while faking sadness in my voice. I open my door and the detective stumbles in obviously drunk and dropping his service revolver. He stumbles into the bathroom to retch up whatever cheap whiskey and beer that was his dinner tonight. I picked up his gun and set it on the kitchen table then set off to get the drunk flat foot out of my hair. When I opened the door he passed out on the floor next to my toilet. Now I could have called his superiors and gotten him into so much trouble but I decided not to. Instead I picked him up and set him up sitting at the table with his head firmly down on the table still passed out.

While he was in a deep drunken sleep I carefully took all of the bullets out of his gun. I then decided to as carefully as I could take the lead tip off and pull out the wadding and gun powder while putting just the tip back in. I then loaded his gun back up and brewed some coffee for the soon to be hungover officer. The smell of the coffee must have awoken him since when he looked around he grabbed his gun and bolted out of the door. I watched out of the window as he sped away in his standard issue crown vic. My plan was set. I knew the layout. All that was left was to lay and wait.

That night I hid in his house in the closet of his art room and waited. My heart was thumping like it was that night. I couldn't help but grin when I heard the car pull up but my grin quickly faded when I heard the voice of a female. Another victim? Damn how could i be so stupid. Was there a pattern I wasn't seeing? Was this all at random? I cracked the door open to watch as he led his lady friend into what is soon to be her final resting place. A thought washed over me. I need to know how he does it and get away with it. Would you pass up the opportunity to watch Salvador Dali paint The Persistence of Memory? No. I didn't think so. I waited.

He was suave and charming. He talked the pretty thin blonde into the murder room. Once in there he does it. Like a viper he was silent and precise, one thin stab to the throat. He gets the tub and slides it over while tying her feet up to hoist her upside down. While he was occupied I emerged from the small containment. And place a hand on his shoulder. He jolted around drawing his weapon and pointed it straight at my head. I raised my hands to show I was no harm. Now with labored breathing the realization has set in. He couldn't do anything to me lest he wants his own kind to find out his dirty little secret. " well french it seems we are kindred spirits. You and i" i said in the most calming voice I could muster. "What the fuck are you doing here? French said in a panicked voice. "Don't worry your secret's safe with me. I won't tell your friends and you leave me alone.`` I said in a slightly cocky voice. Of course I'd never tell him that I planned to kill him as soon as I could. We were the same build so I wasn't worried about a fight. Now that I know that he himself is an artist it threw me through a loop.

 Crazy vs crazy wasn't part of my attack plan. So now I have to outwit him. "There ain't gonna be no deal. You have no leverage here. I have the gun and the power" he said through gritted teeth. Oh so it was power he was after. The blonde hookers. The drinking. He was murdering his wife all over. How could i have not seen this. "French I am leaving i won't tell expect to see me again you naughty boy" I said while smirking and walking towards the door. [Click] that was the sound of the gun not being able to fire the empty bullets as i stroll past him making my way to the free world. A stand off only won by poor timing.

From here I knew I had to be more prepared, more cautious and more aware. On the drive home I stopped by a buy here pay here lot to acquire a new unregistered vehicle. Of course the salesmen took my 2018 toyota suv with 20,000 miles on it for exchange of a 1996 ford truck with 200,000 as an even trade, no paperwork required just a title exchange. Since I couldn't go back to my apartment I had to get more creative with my hunt. With a front seat full of energy drinks and greasy beef sticks I wait down the street from my old apartment. It wasn't too long until I fell asleep. Cancer will do that to you. My weekly chemo sessions were catching up to me and fast. I thought I didn't have long. I had to hurry. I woke up some time later with police surrounding my old apartment. A charge led by detective french. I quickly drove out of there and posted in front of his house yet again. I needed to see if he was still living there or if he had abandoned ship like myself. Then it happened. A blonde, thin, beauty knocks on his door.

As she walked in the house I thought to myself. He's Not that dumb. Is he? I waited until he went upstairs with his next victim. Once upstairs I went to his patrol car and checked the locks. Lucky me it was unlocked. Now the first thing I did was pop the trunk open and have a look. Standard cop stuff. Shotgun med bag road flares duct tape trash bags large ax and a shovel. Well standard for him at least. It just occurred to me that I didn't know how he hid his bodies; he must be transporting them. I couldn't follow in my loud ass truck he would have heard me. So I risked it and hid in his trunk but first I took the spare tire out and its tools and put them in the bed of my truck. I hid in the spare tire compartment and fell asleep.

I woke up with a loud thud and weight laid on top of me. I stayed calm. And was alert for the entire 4 hour drive. When he finally stopped he opened his trunk and removed the body but he left the trunk open. Making sure I was very quiet I peaked my head out and found him using his headlights to light up the hole he was digging. I sneaked up to the front of the car and turned the dash cam on. Gently I

wrapped up my legs with my shoelaces
and made it look like they were tied up.
Reaching in the emergency bag I pulled
the seat belt knife out and sliced my own
forehead. Silently I stalked behind him
and pounced.

A struggle happened as I went for the
throat all while screaming [HELP HELP]
at the top of my lungs. [Bam bam bam.]
The sound of a gunshot wrang in my ears.
This was it. I have been shot. Three
rounds point blank in the chest. I fell
against a tree and just slid down.
Defeated. He got real close to my ear to
whisper something scary before finishing
me off. I didn't give him the opportunity .
I took the seat belt knife and drove it as
hard as I could through his chin and into
his brain. His dead eyes told me that I
had won. I grabbed his phone out of his
pocket and called the police. While I laid
there awaiting deaths next adventure. But
as it seems death had let's say other plans
for me.

Mortality Part 2.

Don't speak. They are coming to get you.
Soon the medics will take you away and
remove the bullets from your lungs.

An otherworldly voice spoke to me as I
lay on the tree taking my final breaths. I
couldn't see him but rather feel him next
to me. He goes on to say.

Death is cold and slow, especially when
you die like this. The numbness in your
body and weakness in your mind is not
due to shock or blood loss. I do that so
you can more easily come to terms with
your fate. You see when they go kicking
and screaming or even worse when they
run or fight it normally ends in them
suffering a fate worse than myself. Do you
know why I haven't taken you yet?

I fell silent as I felt the cold embrace
grabbing tighter on my body. Sirens are
now getting closer and I can see lights.

Good boy. Don't speak. I need you to live.
While I am impartial and inevitable, I
need you to live so you can do my job for
me. You see there are people in this world
that need to pass. That's when you come
in. kill when i say and who i say and you
will be immortal for the remainder of
time.

I close my eyes and nod only to see a
bright light shining through my eyelids. "
He is breathing, we got a live one!" the
paramedics yell out to the team. Then
darkness.

I woke up in a hospital bed with cops
standing around me. My chest wrapped
so tight I could barely move. Undoubtedly
keeping my insides from spewing out. "I
see you are awake, you are a fighter. 3
bullets to the chest and short one lung
and you still wake up." the doctor says
smiling .
" We have some questions for you when
you are feeling up to it. Until then rest up.
We will leave an officer by the door for

your protection" the voice was Kind of off putting for a 7 foot african american sheriff

The questions were as one would assume. With the reaccount I told plus the dashcam footage corroborating my story, they believed it.

Wouldn't you know it? I was officially cancer free. Something about having to remove the damaged section of lung that had the main cluster. Sounds too good to be true but hey. So am i.

Luck was always on my side. I woke up to a nurse changing my i.v fluid. Beautiful and slim. Dead eyes like a shark. Long black hair. No wedding ring. Just my new type.

Angel is her name. She was cold, calculated, and unfeeling. Just like me, she was a killer, just. Like. me. I watched as she changed my i.v bag and went back to checking my chart. Her tell was she went from a plain disinterest on her face to a slight frown. She then scrambles to change my bag to another one and then skulks off. I wonder what that was about. Misread the bags? No. i was going to be another notch in her belt. So the hunt begins again.

Moments after her second switch of the bag there was a tightness in my chest. Like a dump truck had made my heart its own private parking space. Shortness of breath? Check. Left arm numb? Check. Cold sweat? Check. She had slipped something into my i.v. for lack of a better term i've been poisoned.

Remember when I said that luck was always on my side? Just as I was ready to once again pass away the doctors rushed in and saved me right at the last second. Well i was having a heart attack in a hospital already hooked up to monitors. I didn't say a word afterwards. I had found my next hunt.

You know she has killed many people.
She has been doing the worst part of my
job. She has been providing relief to the
people whose time has not yet come. As
you can see she is making my job difficult.
Take the angel of death out.

That familiar deep cold voice is in my ear
again. It's clear now.

Why didn't you tell the doctor what I
did?

The angel of darkness speaks. Funny, I
didn't see her sitting on the edge of my
bed.

What's your game plan huh? You want
money? You wanna fuck me? What do
you want?

Her agitation was the first i've seen her
break. I think I'll have some harmful fun.

Madam i dont know what you mean. I
just suffered the loss of my wife and child,
a house fire, shot 3 times, cancer, and a

heart attack all within a span of one year.
I don't know what you expect me to say. I
just want to rest. Alone.

Don't give me that shit. You looked right
at me. You know what I was going to do.
Until I read your file. You have been
through so much. You are a broken man.
You need healing.

Oh, so she thinks of herself as an Angel of
mercy. I've read about these people. They
get patients close to death but only to
swoop in at the last second and save them.
Sounds like she is addicted to the rush of
being the center of attention. Little did
she know she was about to get all of the
attention she could stand.

Could you please stay with me tonight? I
need to have someone next to me. I feel as
though I need companionship so i dont go
mad.

What the fuck are you talking about? I
can't stay with you tonight. I'm assigning
a different nurse to your room.

She turns to leave on her heels but before she could take a step i gently grabbed her hand and whispered on solid word. A word that is so powerful that time itself stops.

"Please"

She stopped dead in her tracks. The bewildered look in her eyes was only shadowed by the calmness in her response.

"I'll stay. But just for tonight"

I had her. That night we talked about everything. Movies. Art. family. Life's goals and my personal favorite. Past trauma. One night turned to two then three then next thing you know she is helping me upstairs to my apartment door. I'm sure that night was magical for her. We cuddled on my couch and watched a b rated slasher, more of a romantic comedy guy myself, shared our first kiss but was not intimate. Still healing from my injuries. Then she fell asleep in my arms but rest did not find me that evening. Instead a familiar voice echoed in my head.

"Kill her now. She is asleep. Snap her neck and hang her in the shower nobody will know. Blame it on depression"

Death was back and was pissed. Death will have to wait. I want to have fun. This one is special to me.

"Babe go to sleep. You need to rest"

"Yes my darling i will try"

The next morning was a blur to me. I was foggy and light headed. Tunnel vision was becoming of me and I felt weak. My angel was nowhere near me. That bitch poisended me and left. Just as I finished that thought I heard the unlocking of my dead bolt and she walked in. very calm and very caring she whispers.

"Honey, I gave you pain medication to help you sleep. Please stay in bed and get some rest"

Pain medication was her excuse. Typical. Bad news for her was I could not die. I rested my head back and fell asleep. Well not just to sleep but more of a coma. 5 days in my slumber only waking up to occasionally piss and keep hydrated while in the bathroom. I stare down at my toilet and remember when detective french laid down passed out in a drunken haze next to that very same toilet. I miss those days. My own personal angel never left my side except to go to work. Then it hit me. How was she drugging me repeatedly? How was she keeping me in this weakened state? I had to find out and fast.

I stumbled back to my bed and started to rack my brain. Was it the food? No, I was drinking my meals and you have to break the seal before drinking so I know it isn't that. I'd say an I.V but I didn't have one. Possibly injection while asleep? All of this confusion was driving me insane. I needed sleep. I laid down to rest. My rest was disturbed by a soft weight on my chest.

"Morning honey"

"My dear you scared me. How was your day?"

"Fine saved a few people from deaths kiss today but luckily for you i saved a few kisses"

Her playful tone threw me off while she put her soft lips to mine. The taste of her lipstick was metallic and just. Well. off.

" its her lipstick you featherheaded fuck wad. She has been using it to slowly poison you"
Death's voice was ringing in my ears now. He was right. I had to stop kissing her. How do I do that without raising suspicion? Maybe I don't have to. Maybe I can discourage her. I need chapstick. I'll coat the inside and outside of my lips with chapstick then wipe it off when she is

done kissing me. That will at least buy
me some time.

"What's wrong honey?'

She Must have noticed my bewildered
look. I sat up and exclaimed

" i got to vomit"

Tearing through the blankets I quickly
ran to the bathroom and locked the door.
Sticking what felt like my whole hand
down my throat I made sure to purge
everything I had in my system to get
whatever she had poisoned me with to the
toilet. I wretched and heaved until I was
satisfied. Then I washed my face and lips.
Looking into the mirror I noticed my pale
sunken cheekbones and circles under my
eyes that could only describe me as near
death.

I was weak. I needed strength first. I
searched for the chapstick in the medicine
cabinet with no luck. Frantically I started

tearing apart the bathroom searching for my salvation but to no avail.

This clever girl took everything out of the bathroom I could coat my lips with. In desperation I started feverishly brushing my teeth and lips trying to scrub her venom. I then applied some toothpaste with some water to try and give me a minty shield. My only salvation left is a dime store crest.

I walked out of the bathroom and went straight to bed to lay my head on her lap. She smiled that warm smile to me and my heart was swimming. Too bad I had to kill her. She was fun.

"Is my honey still sick"

Her playful yet sad tone rang in my ears as she kissed my forehead in that sweet damn way.

"Yes sweetie, I need to lay to rest. Please go to work. We need the extra money if i am to ever take you on the perfect date"

I whispered while laying my head on my pillow.

"Ok sweetheart give me a kiss"

She said while leaning in towards me.

"Oh no babe i still have vomit smell on my breath"

I said thinking fast. She smiled and walked out the door. I got up and went to the bathroom and grabbed some toilet paper to wipe the kiss off. I take the toilet paper and add it to a plastic bag. Further testing is required. I went to the bathroom and took my old gold wedding ring and laid it on the sink. When I opened the bag the toilet paper fell out and landed on my ring. The gold slowly dissolving tells me its cyanide. It was set. The plan was clear. It was time to act.

LIKE FATHER LIKE SON

I've been in this cabin for a while now, just
by myself and my dog trigger. It has just
been us since momma passed 3 winters ago.
God, I miss her. She always had a way with
things that would make the world seem not
as big as you might think. She always had a
warm smile and better yet always had a
warm meal ready at all times of the day. One
of them few women that can hunt, clean,
and cook. My job was always tending to the
garden for our vegetables and splitting wood
when she needed it. My paw was no longer
with us. Momma said he died out in the
woods when I was just a little baby. I don't
have much to remember him by. Cept of
course an old pocket watch with his and
momma's face in it. Looked like a gruff
handsome man with a blank stare into the
camera. Kind of scary iffn you ask me.

So in the morning I start the day by
checking the traps for critters and birds then
off to chore in the garden. Then after
picking the tomatoes,cucumbers, and corn I
take them in my pack and walk due south to

the river nearby to wash them. Then after
the long trek back with a pack full of food
and a bucket full of cooking water I start
splitting logs for the fire. While splitting
logs on this particular day I heard something
coming from the woods. Sounded like the
footsteps of some critter. Probably a coyote
hopefully not a bear. I ignore it and get back
to choppen.

(distorted animals noise in the distance)

Momma always said if I follow the rules she
has taught me I'll survive in these woods.
1. Never fetch for water at night.
2. Never let the fire die.
3. If you hear something funny. Grab
     trigger and go inside and besure to
     hang snakes skin on the door.
4. Never under any circumstance
     whistle into the woods at night.

Seems like some silly rules to me but
momma lived here her entire life so who
was i to disobey. I grabbed trigger making
sure I hung the snake's skin up like she said
and headed inside. The night was still. No

bugs, no birds. just dark quiet stillness. It
started as a low growl then became a snarl
as trigger leaped up and pointed himself to
our door. Now I replaced that door with 5
half cuts of bog mahogany just this last
summer. Damn thing took forever to shape.
So I know the door is strong. I could hear
whatever it was out there. I could hear it in
my garden. Crushing my ripe tomatoes.
Knocking over a pile of fresh cut wood tha ,
damnit, took me all day to cut.

As fast as it happened it was gone. Trigger
had calmed down some and the night went
back to being quiet. Well figuring I was safe
when I heard the crickets and saw trigger
asleep in front of the fireplace. I threw a few
large logs on the fire and went to bed. I
woke up as soon as the sun peeked over the
valley. Trigger already whining at the door
needed to do his business. When I opened
the door I noticed long footprints in the dirt.

No i aint the smartest man in the world but i
know then something ain't right. The food
prints have only 3 toes on each foot. Damn
things were as big as my arm. Ain't no damn

bear or anything else i had seen or ever saw.
Momma always said that there were critters
in these woods that god had forgotten about.
Did Not rightfully know what she meant
until now. As I was chopping wood I
suddenly remembered that the garden needs
tending too first. Last night had me all sorts
of mixed up.

The garden was as expected destroyed. I had
to rush and find sticks and twine to string up
the tomatoes so they wouldn't be dying any
faster. I got the tomatoes up but revealed
that all of the potatoes and carrots had been
dug up. Didn't know if it was a small critter
or a large one but I had to go check the
traps. Once I got to them they were
destroyed as well. I had to rig them as best
as I could. Couldn't go hungry tonight.
Planned on stew.

Fuck. I needed water for the stew and the
sun was going down. I rushed back to the
cabin and set the bucket on the porch so I
could fetch water in the morning.

"Trigger" "TRIGGER"

No sign of my dog. That husky was old but
he loved to explore. Especially iffin he
caught the scent of something interesting to
him. I grab the ax and bucket and go look
for him. Should have brought a torch. I
could hardly see anything. The moonlight
was only so helpful. It did get brighter when
I reached the river. I kept calling out.

"Trigger!"

Then I did the stupidest thing I have ever
done. I whistled for my dog.

(guttural hissing and growling noise)

The forest went quiet. I armed myself with
the ax and just stood by the bank frozen with
fear. That's when I heard the footsteps.
Slow. pacing and advancing towards me. I
kept still thinking whatever it was out there
it would just get bored and go away. Until I
saw the tallest damn figure. It looked human
from afar

As I got closer I could tell it weren't no damn human. Summ bitch musta been 7 to 8 feet tall. Long scaly arms that swayed side to side with every uneven step. Kind of like he was learning to walk. The face will forever haunt my mind. Looked like some sorta snake but the squeeze kind. Had that long nose and blank dead eyes. He moved slowly towards me and something in me snapped. I rushed to him ax at the ready and swung. Just as I thought I had hit him, I realized. I didn't.

White hot pain instantly threw my body. The monster had grabbed both of my arms mid swing and dug his claws in them. He then picks me up, blood running down my arm and pain shockwaves through my entire body. He brought me face level and hissed out.

"Nice try boy, but you aint your momma"

And with that he lunged for the kill.

(dog barking and growling)

TRIGGER! My loyal to a fault dog came up and bit that old snake thing right on its shoulder. Just hard enough to be let go. Thinking of my dog I picked my ax back up and stuck it in his back. One loud sickening thud later and the monster is back on its knees. Trigger lay next to him whimpering. Sleep well old dog, you deserve the rest and have treated your friend good until the end.

I walk around and face the monster and make him look me in the eye. Then the damn thing started shrinking. The more it shrank the more lifeless it was until I swear to god to this day it changed into a human. But not just any human. My paw. Sure he was older but those eyes. I opened up my pocket watch to be sure. The eyes were the same. That same dead look in his eyes.

I picked the trigger up and took him back home to bury him and dress my wounds. I sat in front of my unlit fireplace and just breathed. Suppose I couldn't help myself but to think.

Like father like sssson

DARKNESS SURROUNDS

Ever wondered what it would be like being blind? Well I did. Let me tell you a secret, it's not worth it at all. Don't do it. Listen to this cautionary tale of my mistakes.

Used to be a scientist and avid christian. I lived in a perfect little world with a perfect son and a perfect wife. Decent house in the suburbs and a nice car and good size backyard. You see, my career was a contradiction in itself because science disproves the existence in all gods of all forms but religion isn't about science it's about faith. Faith in one's eternal damnation of one's soul is something well beyond the comprehension of any mortal. I am getting ahead of myself. Let me start over.

When I was a boy I grew up Roman catholic. If i were to misbehave my mother would lock me in a closet to pray. Now there was a time that terrified me but as i grew older i noticed that the light of god only shines through our darkest of days. The darkness to me would make me feel God's grace. I Craved it as a child and even more now as an adult. I became a Cognitive psychologist, sometimes called brain scientists, studying how the human brain works — how we think, remember and learn. I apply psychological science to understand how we perceive events and make decisions. This of course mixed with my unwavering love for god became a most devastating conclusion.

I spent years trying to connect the link to the human brain to the love of what's holy. How we react when we see imagery of the light and how that direct sight can either sway or turn away from his grace. Then one day it hit me. Sight. When we see the light of god our brains tell us to feel the light instead of just simply feeling it. I started to do testing.

I spent one whole week blindfolded in the sweet sweet darkness locked in my study. My dear faithful wife would bring me food and drink. And for that week my heart swole with ever loving blissfulness that is our god! Then I took the blindfold off. Everything was blinding and hateful. You see when you lose your sense of sight your brain overcompensates and turns your hearing up and well lets just say you are very much aware of everything making noise around you.

3 weeks after i took the blindfold off my life turned for the worst. My boss fired me for my attendance. Took one week off and they said that I should have put a notice in. jance in the front office leaves 10 minutes early every single day and i am the one who gets fired? That's fine, I've made plenty of money in my life. Didn't really need the job. The real shocker is when I came home one Sunday after church I found my loving wife had left with our son. The letter said something about abuse but that harlet clearly has never read the good book. Spare the rod and spoil the child.

Jobless and alone, I could finally reach my goal. Nothing was stopping me from attaining his light and love for all eternity. I sat at my desk in the study looking at the bottle of bleach and eyedropper. I slowly

filled the eyedropper with the burning
solution. As I raised the dropper in the air I
stared at the small hole in the long glass tube
as the one single drop came down and
landed on my cheek.

No, I didn't miss it, I changed my mind at
the last moment. I needed a better plan.
Bleach has too high of a chance of not
working. I run and grab a knife out of the
kitchen and go stand in the master bathroom.
I take my shirt off to not stain it for the up
and coming project. While staring into the
mirror I took the knife and raised it to my
eye and with one quick stab. The left was
gone.

Searing pain shot through my body and I fell
to the floor rolling and writhing. I'm not one
for doing things halfway. In my haste and
pain I lost the knife. So in my panic I found
the nail polish remover. Screaming in
righteous vigor I pour the contents of the
bottle on both of my eyes. I'm burning. Oh
the burning was glorious. I felt the warm
envelope of my body as I went fully
unconscious.. When I woke up I could hear

the doctor explain to the nurse that I was
found by the neighbors who heard me
scream. 3 long weeks in the hospital plus an
additional 4 weeks with an at home
caretaker to help me with my new life as a
blind man.

I sit here in the quietness of my home and I
can hear everything amplified by 1000. The
dog barking down the street, the baby crying
across town, and the drip of the faucet in the
spare bathroom I no longer use but most of
all I can hear the dead. They tell me their
secrets. They tell me how they die. How
they miss the living but most of all i heard
god almighty himself. I've reached my goal
and I regret it all. The mistreatment, the lies,
the righteousness, and the unbinding will of
my religion. After all I have learned this is
the most important lesson I can give. God
has abandoned us. I know. He told me.

Is this love?

7:03am she wakes up from her night of
sleep. I would say beauty rest but let's face
it. She doesn't need it.
7:16 am she gets her work clothes laid out
for the day and undresses for a shower. I
turn my head to give her some privacy.
7:43am she steps out of the shower and gets
dressed for her office job. I still advert my
eyes.
8:04am she makes her way to the kitchen to
grab her breakfast coffee. Oh no she is out
of her favorite brand. Folgers dark roast. She
checks her watch and heads out to the car.
8:08 am she pulls out of her driveway and
heads down the road. I follow her.
8:18am she pulls up to a local coffee shop in
the drive through and orders a large black
dark roast with 2 sugars and no cream.
Strong drink for a strong independent
woman.
8:27am she pulls into her reserved parking
spot to her office job. Just made it on time.

Turning away in my van I retrace the exact route she takes home and park exactly in front of her home on the road. I step out of my van and check the magnet on my door. " safe way pool cleaning" so i pull my fake bucket and skimmer and go into her back yard and walk right up to the back door. Now her pool did not need cleaning. It was perfect just like her. Bending over I grab the fake rock located exactly 3.5 inches from her door frame and gently remove the spare key and let myself in. leaving the key in the door.

Her house smelled just like lavender and vanilla. I bet that's how she smells. Just. perfect. 4 steps then a left turn. I knock on the counter exactly 3 times then open 5 out of the 9 cupboard doors ending on the cupboard with an empty coffee can. I slip a small can of her favorite coffee in the cupboard and shut the cupboard 3 times and then turn left and walk 4 steps then a right turn and out the door. I flick my nail 4 times and shut the door and lock it. Out of the bucket I grab my ruler and measure the rock and make sure it's exactly the way I found it before replacing the key. Then I go back to my van and take a drive.

I circle the block exactly 7 times before checking my watch. 11:45 am time to go back.

12:06pm is her lunch break. Time to see where she goes.
12:09pm she pulls into a subway. Gets her normal 6 inch on flatbread. All veggies, no meat or cheese. She cares so much about others feelings that she doesn't eat meat.
12:13 she pulls out of the drive through and heads back to her office.
12:16 she pulls into her parking spot and removes the bag all while talking on the phone.

Talking on the phone? To whom? Her mom lives 5 states away and the time zones don't match up plus her friends all work with her.

Speaking of time, I have to get back. I park exactly in front of her home again. I go inside and straight to the basement. I shut off all of her drainage pipes and waited.

Paid for a bunch of advertisements about my "plumbing business" as to be the first she calls. Heading home I had to wait at every stop sign for exactly 10 seconds. Honking be damned. I enter my upstairs one bedroom apartment and take 4 steps in the turn left and knock on the counter 3 times and open 5 out of the 7 cupboards I have then go to the refrigerator. Leftover pork chops from the night before sounded good for tonight. I cooked the leftovers for exactly 1 minute and 13 seconds. Then sat down and started flipping through channels and had to skip over channel 45, 76, and 119 twice before settling on some adult animations. After an early dinner. I got to the bathroom.

Flick the light switch on and off 4 times and then take off and put on my shirt twice. Before completely undressing and getting in the shower. Starting the water I pull the thermometer out of the medicine cabinet to be sure the water is a stable 120 degrees and as I was putting the thermometer back I see that my pill bottles are still full. I jump in the shower and spin 3 times before grabbing

the leftmost bar of soap and lather my body
4 times before rinsing off. No need for
shampoo as I keep my whole body hairless.
Hair is disgusting on the body. Hair belongs
to animals. I step out of the bathroom to a
missed call on my cell phone. I turn my lock
screen on and off 7 times before I call back.

I'm greeted by the soft tone of a woman's
voice needing a plumber. Apparently her
drains are clogged. My heart swells with joy
as I tell her I'll be right over. I get dressed
and step to my door making sure to flick my
nail 4 times then off I go. I park exactly in
front of her house and I grab my tool bag
and go to the front door.   When she answers
the door she is in a black silk robe and
shows me to the basement. I "fix" the issues
and she leads me to the front door again.
Then she asks me to go upstairs to check out
the toilet.

I feel weird going upstairs. Like this is all a
dream. I grabbed my wrench and made
myself ready. She opens the door and I walk
in. panic and confusion. The walls are lined
with pictures of me! Red thread detailing my

every stop and even some pictures of me
sitting out front of her house and me in my
house? The detail was amazing. Quickly I
turned to face her wrench at the ready but to
no avail. I was now staring down the barrel
of a loaded gun. One quick bang and my
lights were off forever. Now it's just
nothing. Just silence and warmth of my
blood covering my body while I lay
bleeding on the floor. I couldn't die like this.
I flick my nail 4 times. Now I can rest.

Sleep well

Have you ever had insomnia? I don't mean 1
or 2 days of consuming red bull and coffee
and going on a 27 season tv binge because
"you can't sleep" i mean real insomnia.
Where you lay in bed and stare at a wall
only to get maybe 20 to 30 minutes of sleep
at a time. Staying up for 5 days straight
while feeling no exhaustion and then when
the inevitable crash happens you only sleep
for 1 hour and you are back to no sleep.

I actually have insomnia but not because of
some neurological disorder oh no. It's
because I have a sleep paralysis demon.
Every night I laid in bed and it would sit on
my chest just staring into my eyes just
inches from my face. I couldn't move and
could barely breathe. The smell of its breath
was like rotting flesh and a hint of cherries.
Wait, cherrie? I don't even like cherries. I
understood the rotting flesh but cherries.
Was this not in my head? Was this little shit
real?

The next night I set a trail of cherries out to a bear trap hoping to catch it. Not knowing where it comes from, every night I had to make three possible trails. And every morning I'm sweeping rotted cherries off the floor and throwing them away in a nearby trash can. I tried new paths but still the same results. Rotted cherries into an empty trash can. Wait empty? I haven't taken the trash out yet? Does this little shit like rotted cherries? New plan is to arm the bear trap at the bottom of the trash can then place a pile of rotted cherries.

The next day the trap was set and I left for the evening thinking to myself that I needed a break from well. having a mental breakdown. So I decided to go out to a local bar and try to get so drunk I just passed out for days. The bar I favor is this little hole in the wall place two blocks from my house with a gruff old bartender who can pour the coldest glass of piss water you have ever tasted. Hey for a dollar a glass just be glad it wasn't actually piss. Just shitty beer. Walking in I see the familiar neon beer sign and smell of cigarettes and stale peanuts.

Although there was something new. She was new.

As I sat at the bar and ordered the house piss she served me with a smile. Which I think is the first smile I have ever seen in this particular establishment. She tells me her name is Alex and she was just hired to help out the old gruff bartender. She's cute and I start mildly flirting and wouldn't you know it she responds with light flirting back. I think she was just being nice to earn a tip. 6 more beers later I tip double and stumble back to my house completely forgetting about the trap.

Reaching my door I heard the sound of what I could only describe as if a mouse was caught in a trap but the mouse was voiced by darth vader. Deep and breathy. In my drunken haze I ran to the trash can tripping and knocking it on its side. Inside I could see this well. Thing. Huge black eyes with a wide grin filled with rows of sharp teeth that looked to be blood stained. Thinking about it now it might have been cherry stained. Then I smelled the stench of rotting flesh and my whole body went numb. I couldn't move only stare into its big empty eyes. He lunged after me but stopped halfway, having his leg trapped in the beartrap.

All night I stared at him. He just snarled at me. No sounds, no movement, he just sat in the overturned trash can and stared at me. When the sun finally came up he retreated further into the can and I could move again. I sat up and scooted back to the wall behind me and sat there looking at him. What the fuck are you. I said to myself. Without prompting he looked at me and said something I wish I had not heard. "Nhag, i Nhag not a thing just Nhag".

"Jesus Christ you fucking talk" i screamed as i jumped to my feet looking for something to defend myself with. "Ahhhh no name. Name its hurts' ' it wallowed in the can. So saying the lord's name hurts it? What the actuall fuck was this little gremlin reject? I grabbed the corner lamp and used the base to flip the can right side up. Nhag tried to jump out but the sunlight burned his skin as soon as it touched him. A loud scream slates his body in pain. Well now I know he is a gremlin reject. Wonder if he can eat past midnight or get wet?

Without thinking I ran to the bathroom to grab a glass of water and when I ran back in I poured it on him. He didn't react except by looking at me with a very angry " why did you do that " face. Sheepishly I apologized and sat at the foot of my bed just staring at the trash can. I don't know what to do. "What do you want from me?" I said more under my breath. Defeat in my voice.

"I eat sleep, can't go hungry, can't go home" his voice was like nails on a chalkboard to my ears. High pitched yet somehow gargled at the same time. Not being able to comprehend what he has just said. I tried to lay down to get some sleep. Completely forgetting I have a job and responsibilities. Oh well I guess there are more pressing matters. After a quick nap of course. When I woke up it was night time. 40 missed calls and just as many texts. Guess I have to look for a new job. I check the can and Nhag is asleep in there so i decided since he isn't

going anywhere i go out and try to clear my
head.

Walking down the street I found myself
standing in front of the same bar I was at
just a few nights before. I step inside and sit
at the bar and Alex shows up behind me.
She tells me she is not on her shift and was
taking advantage of her discount. She sat
next to me and we talked and drank and
drank and talked and somehow we wound
up making out and jumping in an uber off to
my house. My drunken lust will be my
ultimate downfall.

The passion was great. Despite me not
having sex for the better part of 2 years it
lasted hours. While I was on top of her I
heard the trash can fall over and the
bedroom door open and close. I stopped mid
thrust and went to take a look back but her
begging for me to keep going kept my
drunken mind motivated.i didn't notice the
red and blue lights shining through my
window. I didn't notice the bedroom door
wide open. And i didnt notice holding the
butcher knife but I did notice alex. Her neck

opened and blood gushed out by the gallon. Her cold dead eyes told me I had done something horrible.

The next few months were a blur. The arrest. The trial. The sentencing. All of it. From what I gathered the neighbors called the police due to screaming. Probably confused with moaning. It's not so bad though. 3 meals a day. Solitude and I get to work out 1 hour a day. The best part is I sleep like a baby now. I've never been so rested. Unfortunately all good things come to an end and today is the day. I lay on the hospital bed and await the injection. I could feel the spectators burning a hole in my face with their glares of hatred. It was deserved. I lay back and closed my eyes and that's when I smelled it. Rotten flesh and cherries. I opened my eyes and there he was. Sitting on my chest with that fucking toothy smile.

My last sight was him. My last feeling was the crushing realization that I was in fact innocent. Before I lost my consciousness he had only one thing to say. " sleep well"

Hunger.

I am just an everyday type of guy. Average
C student. I've never been one to stand out
in a crowd. Never had cool clothes or hair
cut or cars. I tried living my life as modestly
as possible. That is until I got into college.
While studying in general studies I
consumed copious amounts of booze all
while racking up multiple debts including
credit cards and student loans. One dumb
choice after another but hey that's life i
guess.

Post graduation I had a hard time finding a
job that required my degree. I did however
land a job at our local grocery store. It was
the only job I could get that was above
minimum wage and I could support myself.
You see my parents died while in college
and since my grandparents died before I was
born and I have no aunts or uncles and no
brothers or sisters I had to front the whole
funeral cost. My mom was a gas station
attendant and my father owned his own
mechanic shop so they had no life savings to
speak of and no life insurance. Just run off

the mill blue collar workers. Suppose if they had any other skills or the ability to put the damn cigarette down they would have smelled the gas leak in the kitchen. One last spark to forever end their addiction. Rest in peace i guess.

The days go by and I grow weak. Can't remember the last time I ate. I try to eat 3 meals a week. In between working 12 to 16 hour days stocking shelves and the need to sleep I rarely find time for food. You would think that working so many hours and only living in a shitty studio apartment would have plenty of money but I don't.

School debt, credit cards, and funeral debt went unpaid for so long that it's being garnished from every check until the balance is paid off. I have just enough for rent, utilities and bus fare back and forth to work. I tried getting other jobs and better paying positions but unfortunately this town is very limited to inner circle hiring. An inner circle I am not a part of. Every once in a while I'll try to hit up a food bank and every charity I can but that's few and far between. Once a month handouts whenever I can make them only go so far.

It's not like I could eat anyway. Everything solid I eat I throw right back up within five minutes of eating. So I switched to liquid meals to try and get my nutrients. Every morning when I get home I drink a can of insure and go lay on the couch and ignore the pains in my stomach and put some mindless tv on until I fall asleep. Then I wake up feeling weak and go take a shower and get ready for work. The bus pulls right in front and lately I've been getting weaker and weaker. Some days I can't drag myself out of bed. The crippling pain in my stomach paired with getting weaker I find myself crawling to the shower more often.

Work is the same every day but it's getting harder to do. I work mostly alone so I don't talk to anybody all night. I just put my headphones in and drag the skids of food out and stock them. But I'm getting slower. My manager that normally greets me with a smile and wave came up to me and commented on how much weight ive lost and that I look sick. I'd go to the doctor but I don't have health insurance and don't want to go further in debt. Simply, I just can't afford it.

The new trend now is that when i go to eat and inevitably puke i've been seeing black chunks in the toilet. Suppose it has been 4 or 5 weeks since i last kept a meal down. Maybe longer i've been losing time. I know it will be a financial hit but I decided to take a week off of work just to rest. After seeing the black chunks in the toilet I need some time to rest.

The first day I checked the fridge to see what I had to eat. So far I have 3 cans of my liquid meals and everything else is rotten. The freezer was worse. Just empty. Nothing in the cabinet either. Probably a good thing. Don't have the energy to cook anyways. That's when I decided to call for a pizza only for my card to get declined. No shocker there. I grab one of the cans and go back to laying on the couch. I could barely lift the can to my mouth let alone drink it but I had too. Whatever this bug was needed to go away so I can get back to work. I check my phone every five minutes to see if my latest paycheck has been deposited but nothing so far. Suppose I could skip on the water bill this month and use my 20% discount on groceries from work. It's not a lot but it's something.

When I woke up on the second day I felt like my stomach was turning inside out. The pain was blinding. I couldn't stand or see just pain. Ever had hunger cramps? Try having them while getting punched in the gut. I crawl to the fridge again and open it only to find the fridge is warm and my last two cans are warm and spoiled. Great, that's all i need is to have my pos refrigerator go out. Perhaps if I just lay on the cold tile floor for a bit I would feel good enough to go to bed. I woke up in a haze and covered in bile and blood? I summoned all the power I had left in my body and drug myself to the couch. I laid down and grabbed my phone to call for help. Fuck how long was i out? My phone was dead. I plugged my phone in and held the button down to turn it on. To my surprise it turned on and I was feeling a little better. And I got paid. In my lapsed judgment I called my local pizza parlor and had one large pepperoni sent to me. I lay back and smile, finally feeling good enough to eat. I could hear my mothers voice calling in my head. I could hear her calling for me. I closed my eyes and now I can see her. I've been reunited with my mother and my father in my dreams. My only question is. When do I wake up? I have a pizza coming.

The Interview.

Allen:

Where am i? It's so dark. It's so quiet. Why
am I sitting in the chair? Hello? Is there
anybody there?

Devil:

Yes allen whipman wasn't it? How are you
doing, young man? I trust that you are well?

Allen:

Who the fuck is that? Who is there? I swear
I didn't do anything!

Devil:

OH my mistake, how thoughtless of me.
Let's shine some light on this.(Two claps
thunder in the dark)

Allen:

Oh shit oh shit. Ummm silver desk. Uh 5'10
white male. No facial scar. Medium black
hair. Small curly mustache. Black eyes.
What the fuck black eyes! Ummm
ummmmmm. Last seen wearing a brown

duster over a yellow polo and black dickies flat creesed in the middle. Brown wing tip shoes. Deep soothing voice……

Devil:
(Interrupting Allen) What are you doing my dear man? Have you gone mad already?
Allen:
No you sun of a bitch! It's one of the first things we teach kidnap victims at the academy. Thats right you stole the wrong mother fucker. I am a police chief you dipshit. My boys will be here any minute to bust your ass. Let me go and I'll be sure the only ass whooping you get is from the court you shit!

Devil:
(with a low rumbling laughter) oh my you still haven't figured it out yet have you? Well "chief" Allen, let's get to why you are here. Just let me pull out my list here. Hmmm yes let's start with how you threw your old chief under the bus during a high stakes sex trafficking ring and had the whole thing pinned on him.(clicks tongue) not very nice i'm afraid. Oh and we can discuss the

fact at said event you went from rookie to detective overnight. How fortunate it is for you but unfortunate for the young men you have thrown into jail while planting drugs on them to further push your career and what was that comment you said to your short lived partner who discovered you? "It doesnt matter they were niggers? Oh my allen such predigest towards a community based on skin color (clicks tongue) i'm afraid i haven't even begun.

Allen:

Oh I see what this is. What are you? FBI? Interpol? Which section do you work for? I didn't do any of those things. I put bad guys in jail. I make the city a safer place to live! I am a goddamn hero! Do you have any idea what will happen to you if you try to pin any of this on me? The public will be furious and will have your ass! Torch and pitchforks! TORCH AND PITCHFORKS MOTHER FUCKER!

Devil:

Yes, well. I can assure you I am none of those things. Let's continue shall we? Your

ex wife knows the one that died in her sleep.
We both know the truth that you killed her.
One quick injection and she dies peacefully.
Let's discuss why you did that shall we?

Allen:
How the fuck did you know that? How long
have you been following me? Ill kill you
mother fucker. Uncuff me and lets go you
fucking pussy!

Devil:
Allen ,sir, you are not shackled in a mortal
way. Think of it in a more spiritual sense.
Like the guilt of all of your sins slowly
sitting on your lap. You are more than
welcome to stand up anytime you want and
leave. Providing of course you can lift the
guilt above your head and walk with it on
your soul. Are you strong enough to do that
allen?

Allen:
What are you? Why am I here? What is this?
Devil:
Finally you have asked the questions that
require an answer.I have many names but

you may call me satan or old scratchen. I do like that one. You are here because the illegal raid on a downtown warehouse got you shot. And this is hell. Oh Allen it was all obvious you dullard.

Allen:
But but. I'm a hero.I saved lives. And how dare you judge me! Isn't the old saying only God can judge me? Last i checked daddy kicked you out of his house because you threw a temper tantrum because he made me in his image so from the image of daddy go fuck yourself.

Devil:
HAHAHAHA thats right Allen god may have made you in his image but much like daddy himself neither can face themselves in the mirror knowing there true image is staring back. I was the exception. Plus I didn't make you do those horrible things. I claimed your soul when you decided that the flesh of the innocent was more tempting than the flesh of the mare. Oh dear you look stunned let me spell it out. Your soul was mine to claim when you decided to fuck

your daughter while your wife watched in disgust from the bedroom door. You know the door to your daughter Emily's room. So lets recap. You are a child rapist, a liar, a murderer, woman abuser and embezzler, and so on and so on. So for you to sit there and judge me is laughable compared to you i am a saint. I am only guilty for knowing and accepting what i am.

Allen:
Is this punishment for my sins? Because you have to step your game up you dickless coward.

Devil:
My good man this isnt your eternal torture. This is your job interview. You see the demons here were not merely conjured up by me. I have to recruit them and well convince them that they have a new purpose. Something larger than themselves. I saw your resume and I had to speak with you myself.

Allen:

Fuck and the sky you fell from. I can take
whatever punishment you throw at me. In
life i was the baddest mother fucker and in
death i am

Devil:
IN DEATH YOU ARE A SPINELESS
WORM. Allen, understand while I have
your soul which is for the rest of eternity i
control how much you feel. Your torture.
Your very existence belongs to me. Sign this
contract and you will have that freedom
once more!
Allen:
I….. I can't sign. I'm a good person. I uphold
the law.

Devil:
The law of man has no bearing on the soul.
So "good person" in your own opinion the
man who stole bread to feed his starving
family is just has bad as the man who fucked
his daughter yet ive never seen you at a
bakery. Pathetic attempt at superiority. Sign
the contract and become "uhlzauge demon
of fault" rise to punish those whom have
faulted you.

Allen:
Fine ill sign. Just stop with this interview. I can't take it. Make me a demon. Ill be the best fucking demon in your black army.

Devil:
Wonderful. Looks like everything is in order. Well get ready your shift starts in 100 years time. As per the contract you must pay your debt of your sins. Oh don't look so bothered. Just think of it this way. When you are done paying your debt will be the same time as your wife that you killed. Perhaps you can find love in the dark. Toodles allen see you in 100 years

Allen:
(screams that fade out into nothing)

Autopsy 23

Recorder turns on

Patient is one mr *beep* age is 79 years old
weight um well 358 lbs height is well this
can't be right 5 foot 3 inches. Well typo
aside. This is dr *beep* I will be the
pathologist for this autopsy. Time is 3:45 am
in this month of June and the day of 10 1990
i will record every word spoken during the
autopsy as per the request of the detective in
charge.

There seems to be no visible lacerations on
the neck or face. The chest is small with
signs of malnourishment despite the very
swollen belly. Arms are set with rigamortis.
No known breakage but the hands are
bruised and swollen. Excuse me, I must go
back to my files.

Let's see. Says here that this gentleman was
a quadriplegic for the past 50 years due to a
drunk driving accident. Poor guy lost his
young wife and was forced to spend the rest
of his life in his thoughts. When will people

just not drive while drinking? Would have saved him a lifetime of misery.

This still doesn't explain the bruising on his hands. Let's continue. Feet have signs of blood pooling in the heels. Common for a man of his condition. Legs are very skinny and lack any defined muscle. Genitals are of normal color, shape, and size for a man of his age.

From the looks of it he has had a shave or a haircut in a while despite his nails being trimmed. Back to the file it says he has been in a healthcare facility for 29 years then moved to a nursing home for the remainder of his life. No known living family. Poor bastard spent his whole life alone. Forgotten.

Well let's get to the fun part. Where did I put that scalpel ? ah yes here it is.making the first incision. Starting at the right collar bone and cutting down towards the end of the sternum. First incisions is done. Now for the second incision on the left collar bone conjoin the two incisions.

WHOA! I must be seeing things. I swear his hand just moved. His nervous system is completely wrecked; he shouldn't have moved in a very long time. I wonder if anyone has seen this before? Going back to file. His medical records indicate he hasn't spoken or showed any traces of consciousness aside from the traced eye movement and blinking in response to questions.

The note in here says he had a pretty nasty bedsore on the back of his neck that never fully healed and that's why he was moved into the nursing home for 24 hour care. Checking the lower half of his neck. I have never seen a bedsore this bad before. Hole is inflamed and red in color. A clear liquid is oozing from it. Collecting the slim substance for further lab testing.

That's weird. His eyes are closed. Note the subject's eyes were open on arrival. I don't think he is dead. I must be cracking. Why couldn't this wait till the morning or even better, afternoon? There is an attached police report. It says here the subject was

involved in the homicide of no less than 6
members of the nursing staff? This can't be
right. Says his fingerprints were found on all
of the victims throats and that there were
two puncture wounds on the nape of the
neck. Victims were paralyzed while he
strangled them to death.

This is absurd. This man doesn't have teeth
let alone vampire fangs. Well according to
the file his teeth were lost in the accident. I
will humor him and check his mouth.
Grabbing the prying vice and inserting the
ends into his mouth. The vice wont turn.
Ugh that was the most sickening crack I've
ever heard.

No Fucking way! There seem to be two.
Well. fangs. But not human. They almost
look arachnid. Oh my sweet lord in heaven
what is that thing! It's coming out of the
bedsore. HELP! HELP! I can't escape its
growing larger.

Detective French, this is my last statement.
This is no man. Roughly 7 feet tall 4 thin
and hairy legs just shot out of his neck. This

thing is were his body like some sort of sick
camouflage . if you get this message. Burn
this building to the ground do let it lay eggs,
we can't be saved!

(screaming engulfs the room drowned out
by the gurgling and cracking of bone then
silence.)